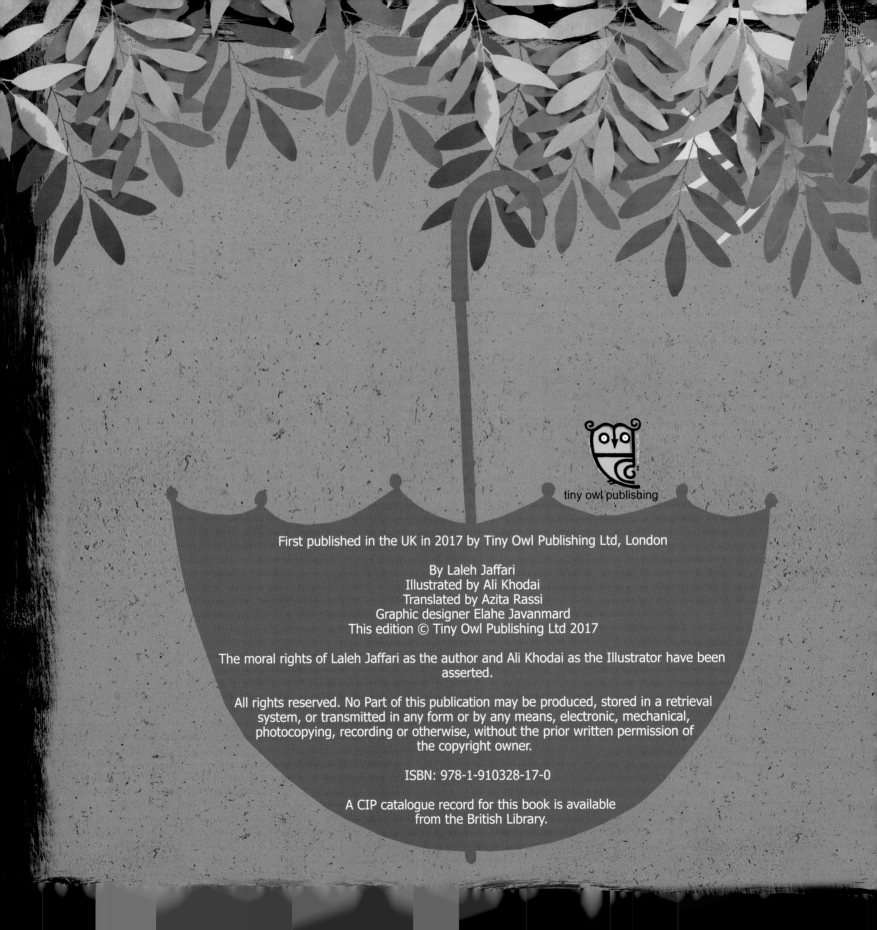

tiny owl publishing

First published in the UK in 2017 by Tiny Owl Publishing Ltd, London

By Laleh Jaffari
Illustrated by Ali Khodai
Translated by Azita Rassi
Graphic designer Elahe Javanmard
This edition © Tiny Owl Publishing Ltd 2017

ISBN: 978-1-910328-17-0

A CIP catalogue record for this book is available
from the British Library.

The Elephant's Umbrella

Laleh Jaffari
Ali Khodai

The elephant loved his umbrella. Whether it drizzled or poured, he'd open his umbrella and walk into the rain, proud to ask anybody he saw to join him under it.

One day, when the elephant was sleeping, the wind swept his umbrella away and gave it to the leopard.

As soon as the leopard saw the umbrella, he said, 'What a lovely umbrella! Will you be mine?'

'If I become yours,' asked the umbrella, 'Where will you take me when it rains?'

'I'll take you hunting with me!' said the leopard proudly. 'I'll hunt anybody I see. And then I'll sit under you and eat them.'

'No, no!' replied the umbrella. 'I'll certainly not belong to you.'

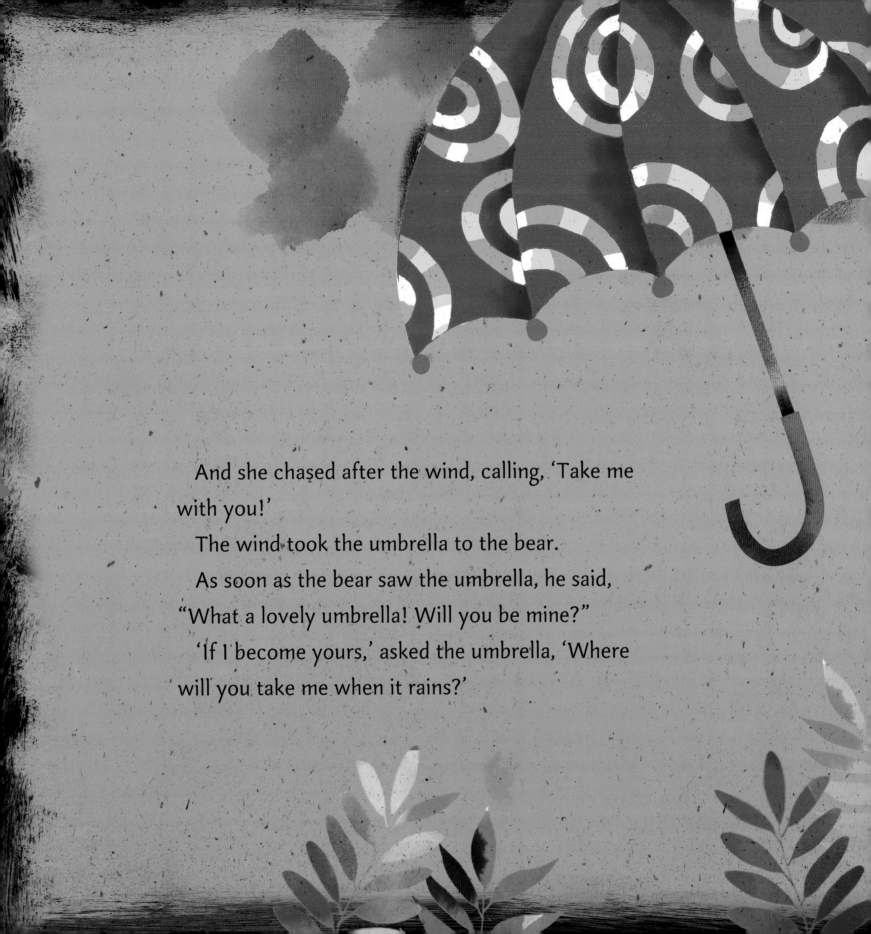

And she chased after the wind, calling, 'Take me with you!'

The wind took the umbrella to the bear.

As soon as the bear saw the umbrella, he said, "What a lovely umbrella! Will you be mine?"

'If I become yours,' asked the umbrella, 'Where will you take me when it rains?'

'I'll take you to the bees,' said the bear. 'I'll take their honey. And then I'll sit under you and eat all that honey by myself.'

'No, no!' replied the umbrella. 'I'll certainly not belong to you.'
And she chased after the wind again.

It was just starting to
rain again and the
umbrella looked
everywhere for
the elephant.

She finally spotted him looking for her. She span over his head so he could see her.

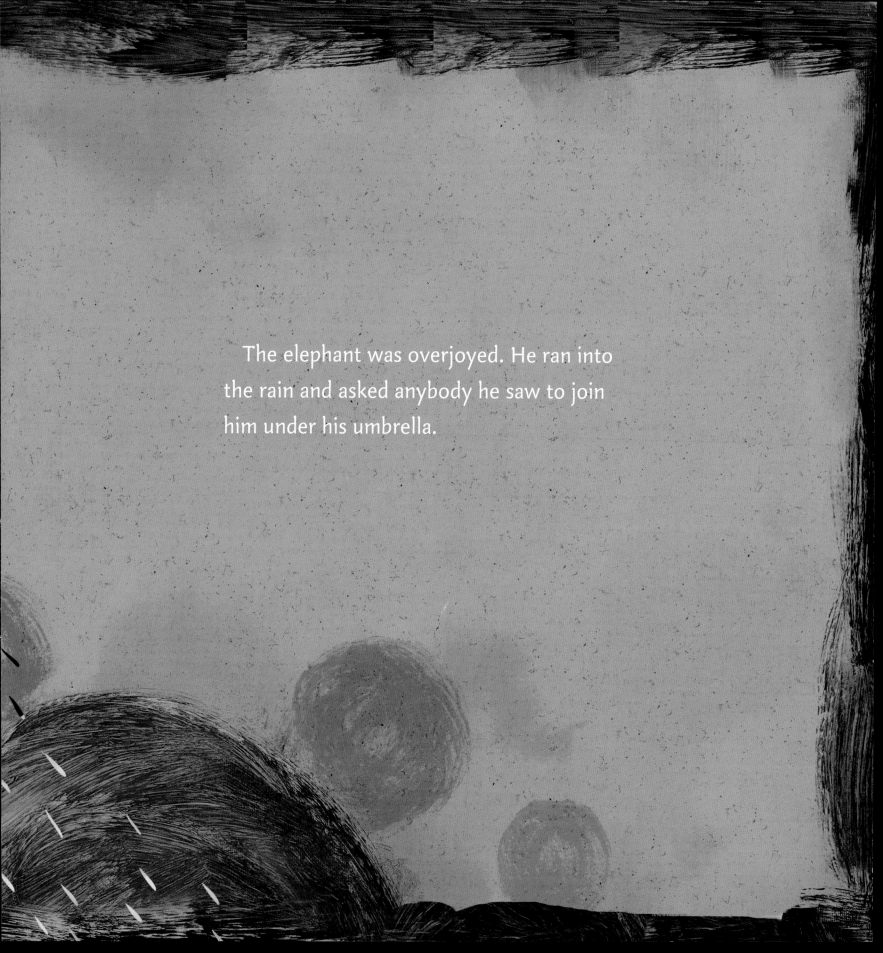

The elephant was overjoyed. He ran into
the rain and asked anybody he saw to join
him under his umbrella.

About the book

The *Elephant's Umbrella* is a simple yet sophisticated tale about how generous we can be to others. The leopard and the bear think only of how the umbrella will make it nicer for them to hunt and eat, while the elephant wants to share the shelter the umbrella provides with his friends. Perhaps it's useful to observe that the elephant's enjoyment lies in sharing.